# MR.CHEERFUL

# MR. CHEERFUL

by Roger Hargreaves

WORLD INTERNATIONAL

Mr Cheerful always woke up in a
cheerful mood, with a bright
sunny smile on his face.

In fact Mr Cheerful was one of the most
cheerful people you are ever likely to meet.

He did, however, have one secret
that made him sad,
but nobody knew about it.

Not yet, anyway.

All I can tell you is that he liked to
keep it under his hat.

Mr Cheerful was never without a smile.

From breakfast time in the morning …

… to his bath time at night,
Mr Cheerful beamed from ear to ear.

He was even happy when it rained.

And on a sunny day,
his smile was even brighter and sunnier
than the sun.

Everybody around him couldn't help
but feel cheerful.

Even the flowers smiled when Mr Cheerful walked past.

When Mr Funny met him, he felt so happy
that he pulled an even
funnier face than usual,
making Mr Cheerful laugh out loud.

Then one day, while out for a walk,
Mr Cheerful bumped into Little Miss Splendid.

Mr Cheerful smiled his usual cheerful smile.

Little Miss Splendid began to smile,
but then she stopped, and looked sternly
at Mr Cheerful.

"How rude!" she exclaimed.
"Young man, don't you know
that you should raise your hat
when you meet a lady!"

For the first time in his life
Mr Cheerful lost his smile.

And then he blushed, bright red!

But he still did not raise his hat.

"You should be ashamed of yourself!"
cried Little Miss Splendid.
"Why won't you raise your hat?"

"I'm too embarrassed," replied Mr Cheerful,
blushing an even brighter red.
"Without my hat on I'm not very good-looking
and that makes me sad."

"Really?" asked Little Miss Splendid.
"Let me see."

Mr Cheerful lifted his hat.

And now I'll tell you what his secret was.

Mr Cheerful had the grand total
of only three hairs on his head!

"Is that all you're worried about?"
asked Little Miss Splendid.
"Why, it's your bright sunny smile
that everybody loves, not how many hairs
you have on your head!"

And Little Miss Splendid smiled.

Then Mr Cheerful smiled.

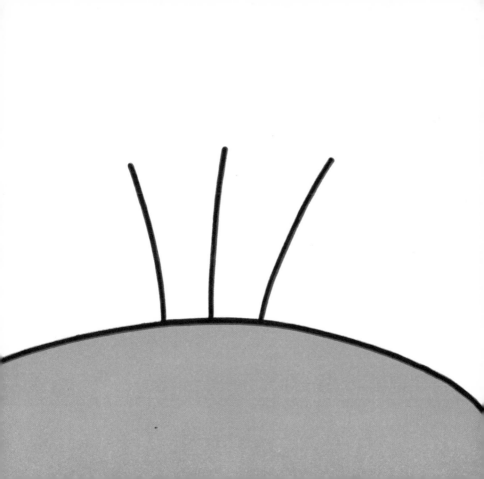

And ever since that day
he hasn't stopped smiling.

And he is always quick to raise his hat
to everyone he meets.

And everyone he meets goes away
feeling happy and cheerful.

Which leaves only one thing
left to say …

… hats off to Mr Cheerful!

# MR MEN question time – can you help?
## 10 sets of 4 Mr Men titles to be won!

Thank you for purchasing a Mr Men pocket book. We would be most grateful if you would help us with the answers to a few questions. Each questionnaire received will be placed in a monthly draw – you could win four Mr Men books of your choice and a free bookmark!

Is this the first Mr Men pocket book you have purchased?  **Yes** ☐  **No** ☐  (please tick)

If No, how many books do you have in your collection?   ___

Have you collected any Little Miss books?  **Yes** ☐  **No** ☐ **How many** ___

Where do you usually shop for children's books?  **Bookshop** ☐  **Newsagent** ☐
**Supermarket** ☐  **Garden Centre** ☐

Would you be interested in a presentation box to keep
your Mr Men books in?  **Yes** ☐  **No** ☐

Do you know that there are other types of Mr Men books?  **Yes** ☐  **No** ☐

If No, would you be interested in knowing about these?  **Yes** ☐  **No** ☐

Apart from Mr Men, who is your favourite children's character? _____

## Thank you for your help.

Return this form to: Marketing Department, World International Limited
Deanway Technology Centre, Wilmslow Road, Handforth, Cheshire SK9 3FB.

Please tick overleaf which four Mr Men books you would like to receive if you are successful in
our monthly draw and fill in your name and address details.

Signature of parent or guardian:
_____

We may occasionally wish to advise you of other children's books that we publish. If you would rather we didn't, please tick this box ☐

Tick the 4 Mr Men books you would like to win.

| | | |
|---|---|---|
| ☐ 1. Mr Tickle | ☐ 16. Mr Noisy | ☐ 31. Mr Tall |
| ☐ 2. Mr Greedy | ☐ 17. Mr Lazy | ☐ 32. Mr Worry |
| ☐ 3. Mr Happy | ☐ 18. Mr Funny | ☐ 33. Mr Nonsense |
| ☐ 4. Mr Nosey | ☐ 19. Mr Mean | ☐ 34. Mr Wrong |
| ☐ 5. Mr Sneeze | ☐ 20. Mr Chatterbox | ☐ 35. Mr Skinny |
| ☐ 6. Mr Bump | ☐ 21. Mr Fussy | ☐ 36. Mr Mischief |
| ☐ 7. Mr Snow | ☐ 22. Mr Bounce | ☐ 37. Mr Clever |
| ☐ 8. Mr Messy | ☐ 23. Mr Muddle | ☐ 38. Mr Busy |
| ☐ 9. Mr Topsy-Turvy | ☐ 24. Mr Dizzy | ☐ 39. Mr Slow |
| ☐ 10. Mr Silly | ☐ 25. Mr Impossible | ☐ 40. Mr Brave |
| ☐ 11. Mr Uppity | ☐ 26. Mr Strong | ☐ 41. Mr Grumble |
| ☐ 12. Mr Small | ☐ 27. Mr Grumpy | ☐ 42. Mr Perfect |
| ☐ 13. Mr Daydream | ☐ 28. Mr Clumsy | ☐ 43. Mr Cheerful |
| ☐ 14. Mr Forgetful | ☐ 29. Mr Quiet | |
| ☐ 15. Mr Jelly | ☐ 30. Mr Rush | |

Your name _____

Address _____

_____

_____ Postcode _____

# 3 Great Offers For Mr Men Fans

**1 Token · EGMONT WORLD**

## 1 FREE Door Hangers and Posters

In every Mr Men and Little Miss Book like this one you will find a special token. Collect 6 and we will send you either a brilliant Mr. Men or Little Miss poster and a Mr Men or Little Miss double sided, full colour, bedroom door hanger. Apply using the coupon overleaf, enclosing six tokens and a 50p coin for your choice of two items.

Egmont World tokens can be used towards any other Egmont World / World International token scheme promotions., in early learning and story / activity books.

**Posters:** Tick your preferred choice of either Mr Men ☐ or Little Miss ☐

**Door Hangers:** Choose from: Mr. Nosey & Mr Muddle ☐, Mr Greedy & Mr Lazy ☐, Mr Tickle & Mr Grumpy ☐, Mr Slow & Mr Busy ☐, Mr Messy & Mr Quiet ☐, Mr Perfect & Mr Forgetful ☐, Little Miss Fun & Little Miss Late ☐, Little Miss Helpful & Little Miss Tidy ☐, Little Miss Busy & Little Miss Brainy ☐, Little Miss Star & Little Miss Fun ☐.
(Please tick)

## 2 Mr Men Library Boxes

Keep your growing collection of Mr Men and Little Miss books in these superb library boxes. With an integral carrying handle and stay-closed fastener, these full colour, plastic boxes are fantastic. They are just £5.49 each including postage. Order overleaf.

## 3 Join The Club

To join the fantastic Mr Men & Little Miss Club, check out the page overleaf NOW!

# Join Our Club!

## MR. MEN & Little Miss CLUB

When you become a member of the fantastic Mr Men and Little Miss Club you'll receive a personal letter from Mr Happy and Little Miss Giggles, a club badge with your name, and a superb Welcome Pack (pictured below right).

You'll also get birthday and Christmas cards from the Mr Men and Little Misses, 2 newsletters crammed with special offers, privileges and news, and a copy of the 12 page Mr Men catalogue which includes great party ideas.

If it were on sale in the shops, the Welcome Pack alone might cost around £13. But a year's membership is just £9.99 (plus 73p postage) with a 14 day money-back guarantee if you are not delighted!

**HOW TO APPLY** To apply for any of these three great offers, ask an adult to complete the coupon below and send it with appropriate payment and tokens (where required) to: Mr Men Offers, PO Box 7, Manchester M19 2HD. Credit card orders for Club membership ONLY by telephone, please call: 01403 242727.

To be completed by an adult

❑ **1.** Please send a poster and door hanger as selected overleaf. I enclose six tokens and a 50p coin for post (coin not required if you are also taking up 2. or 3. below).

❑ **2.** Please send __ Mr Men Library case(s) and __ Little Miss Library case(s) at £5.49 each.

❑ **3.** Please enrol the following in the Mr Men & Little Miss Club at £10.72 (inc postage)

Fan's Name:_____ Fan's Address:_____

_____ Post Code:_____ Date of birth:___/___/___

Your Name:_____ Your Address:_____

Post Code:_____ Name of parent or guardian (if not you):_____

Total amount due: £_____ (£5.49 per Library Case, £10.72 per Club membership)

❑ I enclose a cheque or postal order payable to Egmont World Limited.

❑ Please charge my MasterCard / Visa account.

Card number: | | | | | | | | | | | | | | | | |

Expiry Date: ___/___    Signature: _____

Data Protection Act: If you do **not** wish to receive other family offers from us or companies we recommend, please tick this box ❑. Offer applies to UK only